EASY B CLEMENTE PER
Perdomo, Willie.
Clemente! /

AUG     2010


W 10/13 w4/16

# CLEMENTE!

## WILLIE PERDOMO

### ILLUSTRATED BY
## BRYAN COLLIER

HENRY HOLT AND COMPANY
NEW YORK

**M**y father is the president
of the **GREATEST FANS OF
ROBERTO CLEMENTE CLUB,**
Boogie-down Bronx chapter.
Ask my father why he named me Clemente,
ask him why he thinks that the number 21
should be retired forever,
and he'll start acting like he's a great debater.
He'll take out his baseball card collection
and pull all his mint condition Clementes,
and then he'll start calling Clemente,
I mean really calling him,
like he was trying to talk
to the ghost of Roberto Clemente.

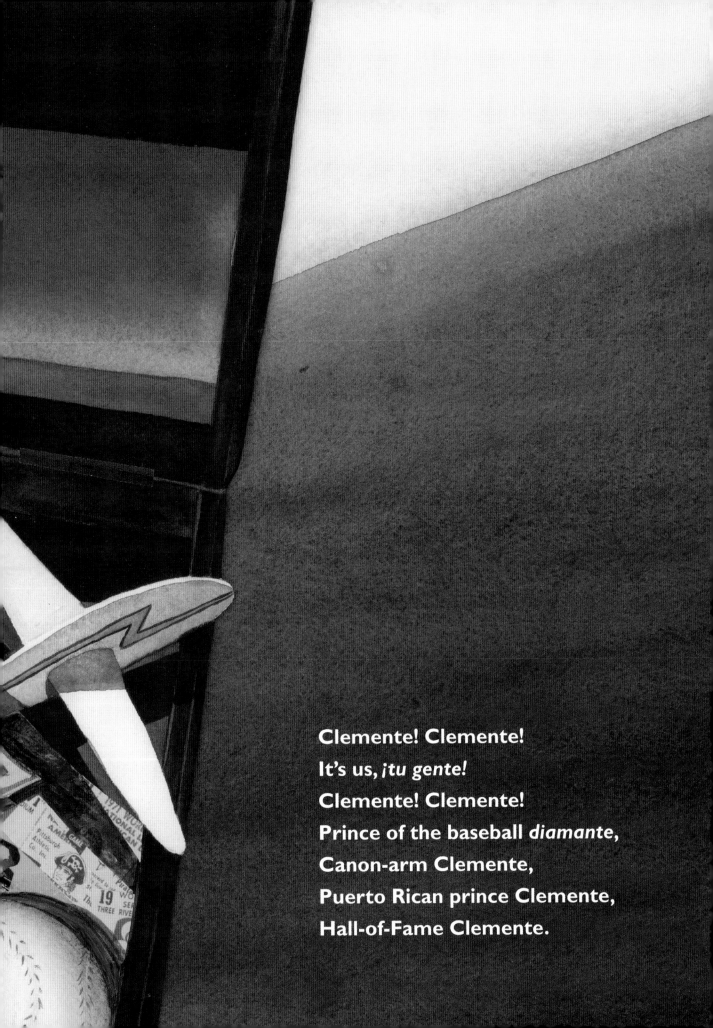

Clemente! Clemente!
It's us, *¡tu gente!*
Clemente! Clemente!
Prince of the baseball *diamante*,
Canon-arm Clemente,
Puerto Rican prince Clemente,
Hall-of-Fame Clemente.

My Uncle Junior,
another **BIG CLEMENTE FAN**,
who wears his Pittsburgh Pirates cap
with his Sunday-church suits—
if he was here he would join my father and say,
"Clemente hit curve balls before they dropped.
Hit fast balls that made a catcher's mitt pop!"
Had a glove like a spider's web dipped in gold—
High-ball hitter
Sinker-ball hitter
Spit-ball hitter
Never-swing-at-the-first-pitch kind of hitter—
Who else got a hit in every game
of the World Series?

Then he points at me and says,
"When your teacher takes attendance,
and she calls 'Clemente,'
you stand up and say,
'¡Presente!' "

For Hero Day at school
I'm going to pick Clemente
because I know all the facts,
I memorized all the stats,
and I can tell you *todo*, everything,
from his rookie season
with the Brooklyn Dodgers
to his last at-bat.

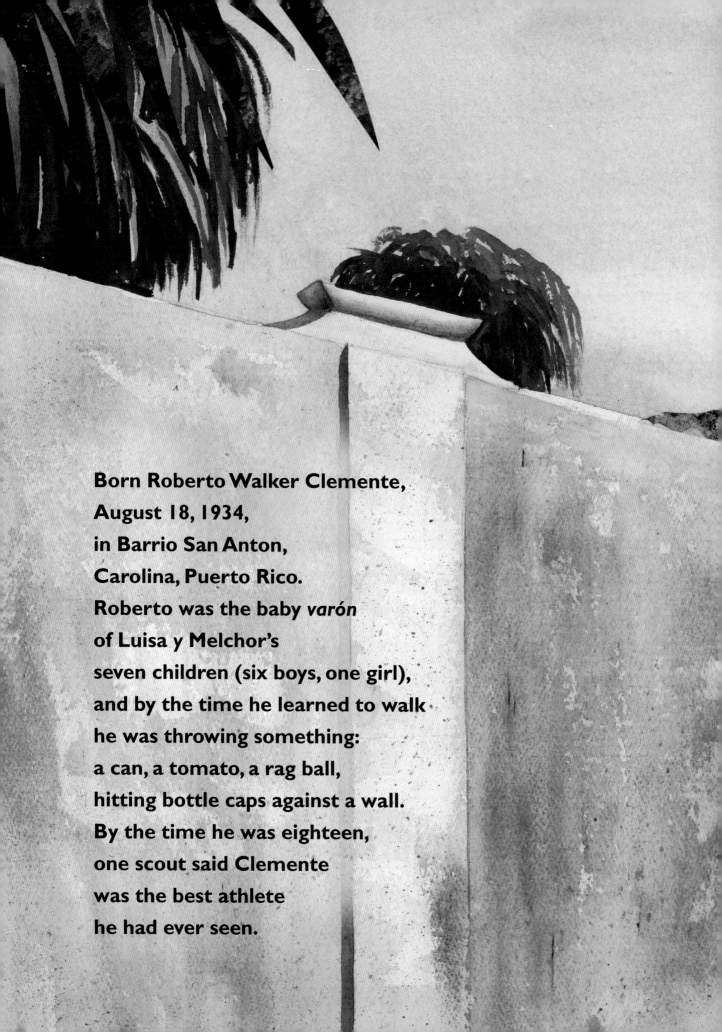

Born Roberto Walker Clemente,
August 18, 1934,
in Barrio San Anton,
Carolina, Puerto Rico.
Roberto was the baby *varón*
of Luisa y Melchor's
seven children (six boys, one girl),
and by the time he learned to walk
he was throwing something:
a can, a tomato, a rag ball,
hitting bottle caps against a wall.
By the time he was eighteen,
one scout said Clemente
was the best athlete
he had ever seen.

4 batting titles,
.317 lifetime average,
came to bat 9,454 times,
got 3,000 hits,
440 doubles,
166 triples,
240 home runs,
12 Golden Gloves . . .

...and a statue
in the Hall of Fame—
Roberto Clemente
was born to play
the game.

And just when you think
you know all about Clemente,
Mami jumps in and reminds us
that he was a good father and a good son because
right in the middle of celebrating the World Series
Clemente interrupted the broadcaster and said:

"And before I say anything in English,
I'd like to say something
to my mother and father in Puerto Rico ..."

On the most important day of my life,

and ask that my parents give their blessing.

En el día mas grande de mi vida,
para los nenes la bendición mía
y que mis padres me echen la bendición.

I give my blessing to my boys

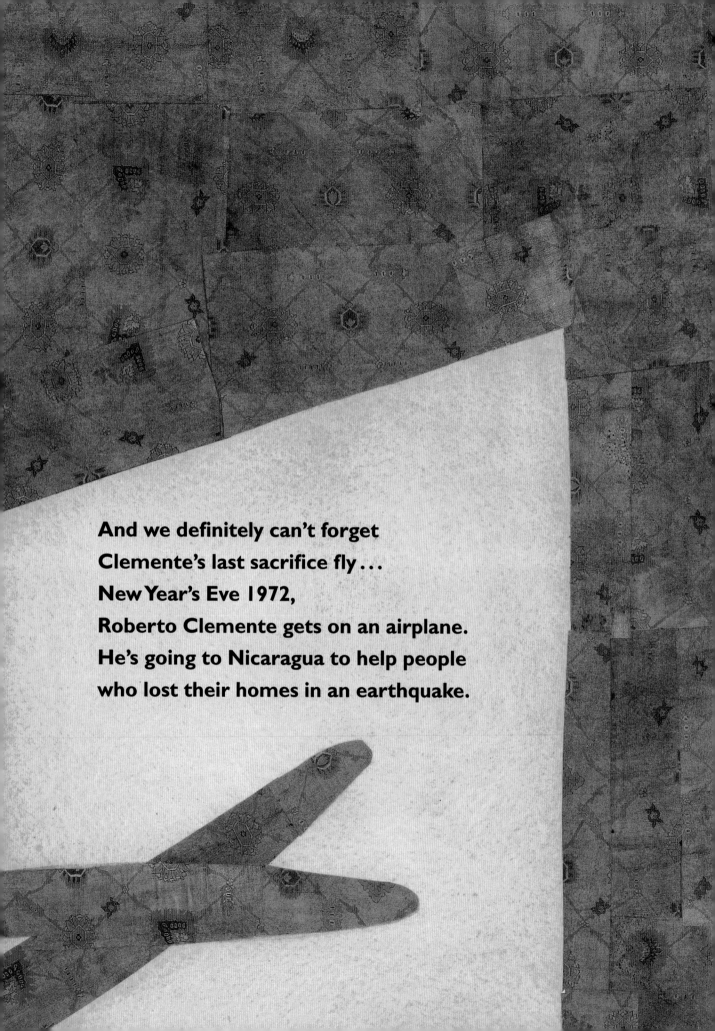

And we definitely can't forget
Clemente's last sacrifice fly...
New Year's Eve 1972,
Roberto Clemente gets on an airplane.
He's going to Nicaragua to help people
who lost their homes in an earthquake.

The plane never got across the ocean.
It was too heavy.
It had too many boxes of food and clothes,
medicine and toys.
The plane crashed into the water,
and Roberto disappeared . . .

His wife, Vera, his three sons, Roberto Jr., Luis, and Enrique,
waited at El Morro, watching the waves for days and days,
hoping that Roberto would come home....
The whole island cried and cried for our hero,
*nuestro tesoro.*

Remember, Mami says . . .
there were days when **Roberto** wanted to quit,
throw his glove away and go home,
because some fans were sending him ugly letters,
and calling him nasty names.
But he never gave up,
*nunca abandonó su sueño,*
and they named bridges and schools after him,
parks and pools after him.

Because he knew that *con respeto*,
*con orgullo*, with faith, with hope,
with belief in yourself, *con valor*,
with standing up for what's right,
fighting against what's wrong,
with love, with keep-on strength,
that anything is possible in this world . . .

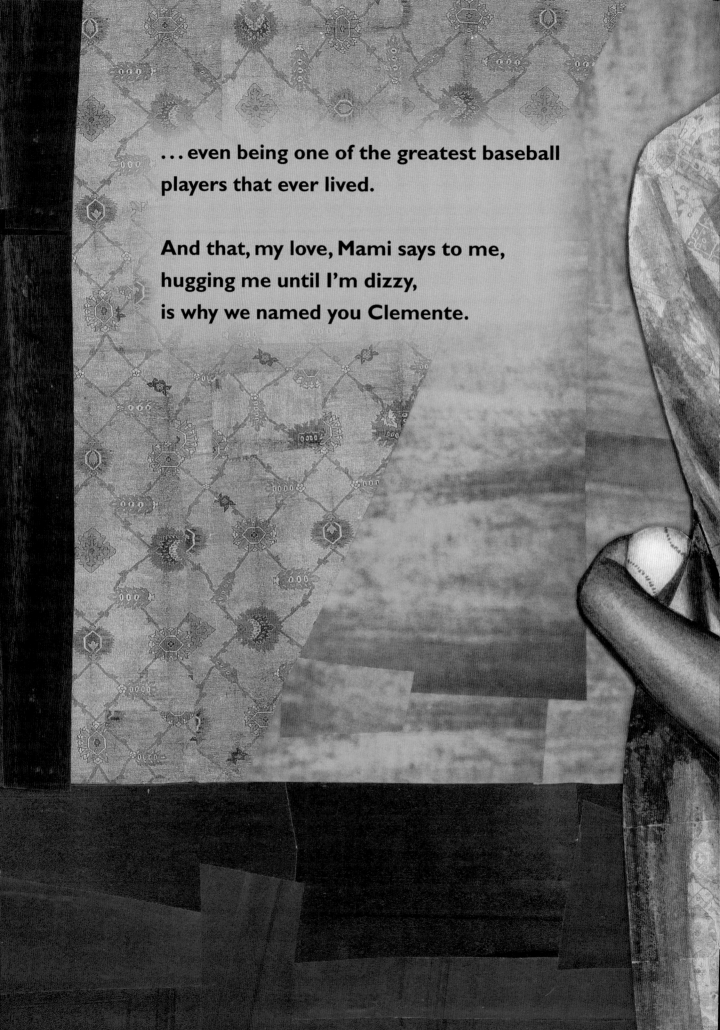

. . . even being one of the greatest baseball
players that ever lived.

And that, my love, Mami says to me,
hugging me until I'm dizzy,
is why we named you Clemente.

# Roberto Clemente Time Line

**August 18, 1934:** Roberto Clemente is born in Barrio San Anton, Carolina, Puerto Rico, to Melchor and Luisa. He is the youngest of seven children.

**Late 1940s:** As a teenager, Clemente often rides the bus to San Juan to watch the Puerto Rican winter league games, where he is able to watch black players from America's Negro Leagues. His favorite team is the San Juan Senadores (Senators).

**1952:** At age eighteen, Clemente signs with the Santurce Cangrejeros (Crabbers) and plays for forty dollars a week.

**1954:** Clemente makes his big break into American Major League Baseball when he signs to play for the Brooklyn Dodgers. Clemente moves from Puerto Rico to the United States. Soon, he is traded to the Pittsburgh Pirates.

**1960:** The Pittsburgh Pirates, once baseball's underdogs, become the National League champions and go on to defeat the New York Yankees on October 13 in a thrilling seventh game of the World Series.

**November 14, 1964:** Clemente marries Vera Zabala, who is from his hometown of Carolina, Puerto Rico.

**August 17, 1965:** Roberto and Vera's first son, Roberto Clemente Jr., is born. Two more sons follow in later years.

**October 17, 1971:** The Pittsburgh Pirates win another spectacular World Series, defeating the Baltimore Orioles in the seventh game. On television, Roberto Clemente gives thanks to his family in a speech in his native Spanish.

**1972:** Roberto Clemente reaches 3,000 career hits. After the season ends, Clemente travels through Latin America. He creates baseball clinics for kids in Puerto Rico and coaches an amateur team in Nicaragua.

**December 23, 1972:** A giant earthquake hits Nicaragua. Later in the week, Clemente decides to fly to Nicaragua to help the people whose homes have been damaged and who are in need of food, clothing, and medicine.

**December 31, 1972:** Roberto Clemente's plane crashes on the way to Nicaragua. His body is never found.

**1973:** Only a few months after his death, Roberto Clemente becomes the first Latino baseball player to be elected to the Hall of Fame. Prior to this event, a player could not be elected to the Hall of Fame until five years after his death.

## Author's Note

In my East Harlem neighborhood, Roberto Clemente was talked about with the same awe and pride as Héctor Lavoe and Willie Colón or Julia De Burgos and Lolita Lebrón were discussed. I didn't know the extent of Clemente's talent until I saw video footage of the 1971 World Series. I remember laughing when Curt Gowdy described Clemente's batting as "vicious." It was the perfect word because during that post-season Clemente sprayed the ball all over the field at will. When I saw him gun down a player from four hundred feet, I laughed again (this time in disbelief) and I had to rewind the DVD to make sure. It's no wonder that Clemente has been compared to aesthetically beautiful things, such as a gazelle or a ballet dancer. His pride, humility, and unrelenting sense of dignity are the best any human being can ask for.

I recently started playing for the Camaradas El Barrio softball team and in honor of Clemente I do not use batting gloves, wristbands, or any other accessories. In today's chemically enhanced sports environment, there seems to be something pure about playing with only a glove, a bat, and a Clincher softball.

## Illustrator's Note

Roberto Clemente's life is celebrated because of the passion and artistry he displayed as a baseball player as well as in his humanitarian work. I created the watercolor-and-collage images of Roberto in action in multiple repeated layers to express the speed, power, impact, and sound he embodied when playing baseball. The other parts of the book show his love of the Spanish-speaking community and fans all around the world. When interviewed in English after the 1971 World Series, in which he was named Most Valuable Player (MVP), he answered in Spanish to his family in Puerto Rico first.

In 1972, Roberto Clemente spearheaded a relief-and-rescue effort to Managua, Nicaragua, which had been devastated by an earthquake. His plane disappeared over the ocean. The people of Puerto Rico stood in prayerful vigil to see if their hero would emerge from the sea. But their noble prince was gone, too soon. The world admires and misses Roberto Clemente because of his service and sacrifice.

# Learn More About Roberto Clemente!

Dunham, Montrew. *Roberto Clemente: Young Ball Player*. New York: Aladdin/Simon and
Schuster, 1997.

Engel, Trudie. *We'll Never Forget You, Roberto Clemente*. New York: Scholastic, 1997.

Márquez, Herón. *Roberto Clemente: Baseball's Humanitarian Hero*. Minneapolis:
Carolrhoda Books, 2005.

## Online:

Go to www.baseballhalloffame.org to view Clemente's baseball stats.

Go to the Smithsonian Institution site at www.robertoclemente.si.edu to see a virtual
exhibition about Roberto Clemente.

Go to www.pbs.org/wgbh/amex/clemente/ to watch a PBS American Experience
program about Roberto Clemente in English or Spanish.

Go to www.mackids.com/clemente to listen to the author read this book.

*For my godchildren: Chuchi, Ashanti, Heaven, and Marc*
*—W. P.*

*I dedicate this book to the Clemente family*
*as well as anyone in need of inspiration—*
*look to the life of Roberto Clemente and you*
*will discover that in order to lead the people,*
*you need to love the people. Inspiration is love.*
*—B. C.*

Henry Holt and Company, LLC, *Publishers since 1866*
175 Fifth Avenue, New York, New York 10010 [www.HenryHoltKids.com]

Henry Holt® is a registered trademark of Henry Holt and Company, LLC.
Text copyright © 2010 by Willie Perdomo. Illustrations copyright © 2010 by Bryan Collier
All rights reserved. Distributed in Canada by H. B. Fenn and Company Ltd.

Library of Congress Cataloging-in-Publication Data
Perdomo, Willie.
Clemente! / Willie Perdomo; illustrated by Bryan Collier.
p.   cm.   ISBN 978-0-8050-8224-1
1. Clemente, Roberto, 1934–1972—Juvenile literature. 2. Baseball players—
Puerto Rico—Biography—Juvenile literature. I. Collier, Bryan, ill. II. Title.
GV865.C439P47 2010   796.357092—dc22   [B]   2009017808

First Edition—2010 / Designed by Patrick Collins
The artist used watercolor and collage to create the illustrations for this book.
Printed in January 2010 in China by South China Printing Co. Ltd.,
Dongguan City, Guangdong Province, on acid-free paper. ∞

10  9  8  7  6  5  4  3  2  1